Daniel Webster Davis

'Weh down Souf, and Other Poems

Daniel Webster Davis

'Weh down Souf, and Other Poems

ISBN/EAN: 9783744711906

Printed in Europe, USA, Canada, Australia, Japan

Cover: Foto ©Andreas Hilbeck / pixelio.de

More available books at **www.hansebooks.com**

"She had lin'ments fur de body,
An' de Bible fur de soul."

Ol' Mistis.—Page 112.

'Weh Down Souf

and other Poems

DANIEL WEBSTER DAVIS

Illustrations
WILLIAM L. SHEPPARD

Cover Design
ELIZABETH GEARY

THE HELMAN-TAYLOR COMPANY
CLEVELAND
1897

To my faithful and affectionate wife

this volume

is lovingly dedicated

by the author.

CONTENTS.

Contents.

'Weh Down Souf.

'WEH DOWN SOUF.

O, de birds ar' sweetly singin',
　　　'Weh down Souf,
An' de banjer is a-ringin',
　　　'Weh down Souf;
An' my heart it is a-sighin',
Whil' de moments am a-flyin',
Fur my hom' I am a-cryin','
　　　'Weh down Souf.

Dar de pickaninnies 's playin',
　　　'Weh down Souf,
An' fur dem I am a-prayin',
　　　'Weh down Souf;
An' when I gits sum munny,
Yo' kin bet I'm gon', my hunny,
Fur de lan' dat am so sunny,
　　　'Weh down Souf.

7

'Weh Down Souf.

Whil' de win' up here's a-blowin',
    'Weh down Souf
De corn is sweetly growin',
    'Weh down Souf.

Dey tells me here ub freedum,
But I ain't a-gwine to heed um,
But I'se gwine fur to lebe um,
    Fur 'weh down Souf.

I bin up here a-wuckin,
    From 'weh down Souf,
An' I ain't a bin a-shurkin'—
    I'm frum 'weh down Souf;
But I'm gittin' mighty werry,
An' de days a-gittin' drerry,
An' I'm hongry, O, so berry,
    Fur my hom' down Souf.

O, de moon dar shines de brighter,
    'Weh down Souf,
An' I know my heart is lighter,
    'Weh down Souf;

8

'Weh Down Souf.

An' de berry thought brings pledjur,
I'll be happy dar 'dout medjur,
Fur dar I hab my tredjur,
    'Weh down Souf.

BAKIN' AN' GREENS.

Yo' may tell me ub pastries an' fine oyster patties,
  Ub salads an' crowkets an' Boston baked beans;
But dar's nuffin' so temptin' to dis gent'mun's palate
  Ez a big slice ub bakin' an' plenty ub greens.

Jes' bile 'um right down, so dey'll melt when yo'
    eat 'um;
  Hab a big streak ub fat an' a small streak o'
    lean.
Dar's nuffin' on urf yo' kin fix up to beat 'um,
  Fur de king ub all dishes am bakin' an' greens.

Den tak' sum good cohn meal, an' sif' it, an' pat it,
  An' put it in ashes wid nuffin' between;
Den blow off de ashes, an' set right down at it,
  Fur dar's nuffin' lik' ash-cake, wid bakin' an'
    greens.

'Twill take de ol' mammies to fix 'um up greazy,
  Wid liker an' dumplin's de bes' you hab seen;

'Weh Down Souf.

Take all yer fin' eatin's—I won't be uneazy,
   Ef you'll lebe me dat bakin' an' plenty ub greens.

Sum folks may lik' tucky, an' sum may lik' chicken,
   But my heart fills wid joy, an' wid pledjur I
      beams,
When I kum home frum wuck an' a day ub hard
      pickin's,
   An' am greeted wid bakin' an' a big dish ub
      greens.

Rich folks in dar kerrige may fro de dus' on me,
   But how kin I enby dem men ub big means;
Dey may hab dispepsy, an' do' dey may scorn me,
   Dey kan't injoy bakin' wid lots ub good greens.

You may put me in rags, fill my cup up wid sor-
      row,
   Let joy be a stranger, an' trouble my dreams;
I still will be smilin', no pain kin I borrow,
   Ef I still kin git bakin', wid plenty ub greens.

KEEP INCHIN' ALONG.

Do' de load be mighty hebby
  An' de road be 'ceedin' ruff,
Do' yer lim's be mighty tired
  An' de paf be dark enuf,
You still mus' keep a-singin'
  To cheer yo' on de road,
" Fur de lane mus' hab a turnin' "
  An' lighter grow de load.
      Keep inchin' along.

What do' de load is hebby
  An' de burden mek yo' sigh,
Jes' ben' yer back a little—
  'Twill be better bime-by;
De cloud's a-hangin' hebby
  Ez yo' journey on de way,
But dar's a silber linin';
  You'll see it, too, sum day.
      Keep inchin' along.

'Weh Down Souf.

'Cause when yo' see de sunshine
 Yo' think erbout de rain,
An' when de rain's a-pourin'
 De sun will shine again.
So tiz wid all de troubles
 Dat dis ol' worl' kin gib—
Do' it rain to-day, to-morrow
 'Twill shine ez shorz yo' lib.
   Keep inchin' along.

Bime-by de journey's ober
 An' heben will hebe in sight,
An' fur all de sighs an' moanin's
 De Lord will mek it right.
Fur de road is gittin' shorter,
 An' lighter gits de song,
An' yo' mos' kin hear de angels
 Ez dey sings a welkum hom'.
   Keep inchin' along.

DE BIGGIS' PIECE UB PIE.

When I wuz a little boy,
  I set me down to cry,
Bekaze my little brudder
  Had de biggis' piece ub pie.
But when I had become a man
  I made my min' to try
An' hustle roun' to git myself
  De biggis' piece ub pie.

An', like in bygone chil'ish days,
  De worl' is hustlin' roun'
To git darselbes de biggis' slice
  Ub honor an' renown;
An' ef I fails to do my bes',
  But stan' aroun' an' cry,
Dis ol' worl' will git away
  Wid bof de plat' an' pie.

An' eben should I git a slice,
  I mus' not cease to try,

'Weh Down Souf.

But keep a-movin' fas' ez life,
　　To hol' my piece ub pie.
Dis ruff ol' worl' has little use
　　Fur dem dat chance to fall,
An' while youze gittin' up agin'
　　'Twill take de plat' an' all.

Yet, ef I fin' my fellow man
　　Don' miss his piece ub pie,
An' dis hard world is standin' roun'
　　To kick him ef he cry,
An' do' my poshun may be small,
　　I'll ack jes' like er man,
An' gib to him a piece ub min',
　　To help him ef I can.

Fur when tiz mine to go alone
　　To de happy hom' ub love,
I kin not take de smallis' piece
　　To dat bright lan' above;
An' when I reach de gol'en gate,
　　In de glory lan' on high,
I'll not be axed how much I had,
　　But how I used my pie.

HOG MEAT.

Deze eatin' folks may tell me ub de gloriz ub
    spring lam',
An' de toofsumnis ub tucky et wid cel'ry an' wid
    jam;
Ub beef-st'ak fried wid unyuns, an' sezoned up so
    fin'—
But yo' jes' kin gimme hog-meat, an' I'm happy
    all de tim'.

When de fros' is on de pun'kin an' de sno'-flakes
    in de ar',
I den begin rejoicin'—hog-killin' time is near;
An' de vizhuns ub de fucher den fill my nightly
    dreams,
Fur de time is fas' a-comin' fur de 'lishus pork an'
    beans.

16

'Weh Down Souf.

We folks dat's frum de kuntry may be behin' de
    sun—
We don't lik' city eatin's, wid beefsteaks dat ain'
    don'—
'Dough muttun chops is splendid, an' dem veal cut-
    lits fin',
To me 'tain't like a sphar-rib, or gret big chunk
    ub chine.

Jes' talk to me 'bout hog-meat, ef yo' want to see
    me pleased,
Fur biled wid beans tiz gor'jus, or made in hog-
    head cheese;
An' I could jes' be happy, 'dout money, cloze or
    house,
Wid plenty yurz an' pig feet made in ol'-fashun
    "souse."

I 'fess I'm only humun, I hab my joys an' cares—
Sum days de clouds hang hebby, sum days de skies
    ar' fair;
But I forgib my in'miz, my heart is free frum hate,
When my bread is filled wid cracklins an' dar's
    chidlins on my plate.

'Weh Down Souf.

'Dough possum meat is glo'yus wid 'taters in de pan,
But put 'longside pork sassage it takes a backward
       stan';
Ub all yer fancy eatin's, jes gib to me fur min'
Sum souse or pork or chidlins, sum sphar-rib, or de
       chine.

FISHIN' HOOK AN' WORMS.

De lubly sky is hangin' wid de clouds ub heb'ny
    blue,
An' de little birds a-wabblin' like dey'd bus' dar
    froats in two;
De gentle kows a-lowin' in the medder 'mong de
    cohn,
While de tree-frog is a-singin' in de fresh an' rosy
    morn;
But ub all de lubly vizhuns dat's floatin' fore my
    min',
De sweetes' is de brook-side, wid fishin' hook an'
    lin'.

When de sun is jes' a-peepin' from its sof' an' balmy
    bed,
While de dew is on de flowers, an' de shades ub
    night is fled,

'Weh Down Souf.

I takes my dinner bucket, when de day is jes'
    begun,
An' I'm gwine off a-fishin' tell de eb'nin' shadders
    kum;
An' 'tain't no use to tell me dat de worl' ain't
    bright an' fhar,
While de kat-fish is a-bitin', and de sun shines
    ebrywhar.

De politishuns tell me dat de votin' is de thing
To put us into power an' de happiness to bring,
But yo' kan't tell me nuffin', 'cause I ain't bin no
    fool,
Sense de days dey had me 'spectin' forty acres an'
    a mule.
Ef dey wants to hab me votin', dey kin bring me
    up to terms
Ef dey'll gib me little lezhur an' sum fishin' hooks
    an' worms.

When de sun is shinin' brightly, jes' erbout de time
    ub noon,
An' de flies ar' lazy buzzin' wid a sweet an' lubly
    chune,

'Weh Down Souf.

I'se a-settin' dar a-noddin', like a scholar wid his
    book,
While de fishes is a-bitin' all de bait frum off my
    hook.
You may say dat I am lazy, 'cause I ain't no
    'risticrat,
But I gwine to hab sum pledjur do', in spite ub
    all er dat.

An' when de slantin' shadders tell de swif' ap-
    proach ub night,
An' de linnet an' de robin quickly homeward wings
    dar flight,
I gethers up my bucket an' de fishes dat I caught,
An' seeks my 'umble cottage ez an hones' fellow
    ought;
So, all de cares an' troubles dat dis ol' worl' kin
    bring
I'll bear widout kumplainin', ef I've fishin' in de
    spring.

SENSE 'KINLEY'S 'NOGURASHUN.

I bin votin' mighty long,—
Thought 'twuz my salvashun—
Now my hopes don' riz right up,
Sense 'Kinley's 'nogurashun.

Feel so good, I boun' to shout
Jes' like all tarnashun,
'Cause we folks don' struck it rich,
Sense 'Kinley's 'nogurashun.

'Bin to Wash'ton, bless yer soul,
To see de 'nogurashun,
'Kinley tol' me, " Jes' keep still, "
Gwine gimme situashun.

Silver bugs look'd mighty sick,
Standin' roun' de stashun,
To see us gent'mun ridin' in
To 'Kinley's 'nogurashun.

22

'Weh Down Souf.

Gwine to sell my ole gray mule,
Rent out my plantashun;
I nebber 'specks to farm no mo',
Sense 'Kinley's 'nogurashun.

Wheat gwine grow on hen nes' gras'—
'Dout no limitashun;
Chickens roos' right on de groun',
Sense 'Kinley's 'nogurashun.

Gold gwine like de goad vine grow—
We'll git 'siderashun,
'Cause we gwine hab all we want,
Sense de 'nogurashun.

Whi' folks now mus' set right back,
In dis mighty nashun;
'Kinley sez our time is kum,
Sense his 'nogurashun.

Wadermilluns gwine grow wild—
Don't dat beat de nashun!
'Kinley tol' me all dese things,
At de 'nogurashun.

'Weh Down Souf.

Tak' hur, whi' folks, lemme kum by;
I wants no botherashun,
Fur dis gent'mun's feelin' large,
Sense de 'nogurashun.

WHY HE SAVED THE ENGINE.

The train was swiftly running, the engineer was
     late—
With greatest speed was running to meet an awful
     fate;
Before it was a washout, which threatened death
     to all,
For none could hope for succor from such an awful
     fall.

Uncle 'Rastus saw the danger, and ran to wave it
     back;
And, in spite of rheumastism, went running up the
     track
Wildly waving his bandanna,— the moment was
     sublime,
Thank God! at last they saw him, and stopped the
     train in time.

When they realized the danger from which they had
     been saved,
Strong men wept and women fainted—they'd been
     so near the grave;

'Weh Down Souf.

Fair hands seized on those black ones, kind hearts
    gave tribute due,
And Uncle 'Rastus stood there, scarcely knowing
    what to do.

A purse was made up quickly, and praise un-
    stinted fell;
How did he come to do it, they all asked him to
    tell.
" You see, de thing wuz dis way: I kum up to de
    scratch,
I didn't want dat ingine tumblin' in my wadermil-
    lun patch.''

EMANCIPATION.

Read at the Emancipation Exercises, True Reformers' Hall,
January 1, 1892.

Blest freedom! 'tis the sweetest strain that fills the
    human heart;
Its blessings doth delight the soul, and sweetest joys
    impart.
The feathered songsters of the grove were mute if
    caged in gold,
And though in rags, the heart that's free finds
    ecstasy untold.

Upon the ocean calm and deep a vessel rides the
    waves,
The freight upon her swelling breast—twenty hu-
    man slaves,
Far from their native land to dwell beneath an
    alien sky,
Far from that dear and sunny land where Afric's
    waters lie.

'Weh Down Souf.

She landed on Virginia's shore, near where we
stand to-day
And gaze upon a lovely group clad all in bright
array.
Memories strong and deep arise, and quick the
tear-drops spring,
As we think of what to-day we are, and what we
late have been.

But yesterday, and dark the clouds that hung above
our sky;
To-day 'tis past and full of joy; the clouds have
drifted by,
The day we longed and prayed for sore at last has
blessed the sight,
And that we come to celebrate—who can but say
'tis right?

E'en in our slav'ry we can trace the kindly hand
of God,
That took us from our sunny land and from our
native sod,

'Weh Down Souf.

Where, clad in Nature's simplest garb, man roamed
     a savage wild,
Untamed his passions; half a man and half a sav-
     age child.

But God, to teach him His dear will, saw fit to bring
     him where
He learned of Him and Jesus Christ those lessons
     rich and rare.
He made the savage into man, tho' moulded by
     the rod;
And Ethiopia has, indeed, stretched forth her hands
     to God.

He was a man and felt as men, his soul with an-
     guish burned;
His heart, too, longed for nobler things, for higher
     missions yearned;
But God still held him to the blast, and still afflicted
     sore
And still he groaned, and still he prayed, yet still
     his burden bore.

But, like the cries of Israel old, his prayers ascended
high,

To reach the great Jehovah's throne, beyond the
azure sky;

His conq'ring power brought freedom down, and
broke the chain, despair,

And bade the Negro walk with men, as free as
Nature's air.

But was he true?   Speak, Bunker Hill, and Boston
Common, say,—

Did he defend from British foe on that historic
day?

While thousands stood with heaving breast, and
dared not strike a blow,

A Negro's voice cheered on the throng, and bade
them charge the foe.

His blood was spilled to gain a place in battle's
honored roll,

And Crispus Attuck nobly stands among the heroes
bold;

And if we speak of valiant deeds, and love of country fair,
Must not begrudge his well-bought fame, but place
  a laurel there.

To-day is hushed the cannon's roar, and peace
  reigns everywhere,
And blessed freedom makes our land the fairest of
  the fair.
Shall we who helped to make it bloom and blos-
  som as a rose,
Be cast aside, unworthy,—our upward course op-
  posed?

We love her and are loyal as the truest of her
  sons;
For her our blood was shed, for her we faced the
  deadly guns.
We'll strive to have her take her place, the first of
  any land;
Stand ready to defend her soil from ev'ry alien
  band.

'Weh Down Souf.

But God has freed us, and to Him we bow in praise
      to-day.
He'll never leave us nor forsake, but will protect
      alway;
And, conscious of a heart that's true, with purpose
      brave and strong,
We'll leave our cause in those just Hands that can-
      not do a wrong.

'Tis the blessing that we celebrate, and not the
      cause now lost,
For that was dear to other hearts as this can be
      to us.
And who were right or who were wrong, we are
      not here to say,
For, still in death, they're heroes all—the blue,
      likewise the gray.

And now, the din of battle past, they are our
      friends the same;
Not such as come to get our votes, not friends
      alone in name,

'Weh Down Souf.

But friends who deep in honest hearts do wish us
 greatest joy.
God grant this friendship e'er may last and be
 without alloy.

Then let us all with one accord now join the ju-
 bilee,
And praise our God who rules o'er this the new
 land of the free,
And babes unborn in future years will rise to call
 us great
For fixing now, for coming time, "The Day We
 Celebrate."

WHEN DE SUN SHINES HOT.

Yo' may talk erbout de snowflakes,
   An' de pleasen' winter breeze;
Ub de pledjurs foun' in skeetin',
   When de ice begins to freeze;
Ub de 'joyments ub de winter,
   Dat yo' think a happy lot—
But gib to me de summer,
   When de sun shines hot.

Dis shiv'rin' an' a-freezin'
   Will nebber do fur me,
Fur when de win's a-blowin'
   I'ze miz'ble ez kin be.
An' jes' erbout November
   I draws up in er knot,
An' don' begin ter straightin'
   'Tell de sun shines hot.

'Weh Down Souf.

But 'long wid frogs an' lizzuds,
 When de sun kums out,
My bones begin er thawin',
 An' I'm ready fur to shout.
Fur de happy thoughts ub summer
 Makes me feel all right,
Fur de wadermillun's kumin'
 When de sun shines bright.

Maybe wuck's gittin' skace,
 An' de meal bag low;
But I nebber feels de trouble
 Ef it is erbout to go,
Fur de good times 's on us,
 An' I 'joys my lot,
'Cause de wadermillun's kumin'
 When de sun shines hot.

Den lemme 'lone, hunny;
 Don' 'sturb dis dream,
Ez I set here a-dozin',
 De field's gittin' green,

'Weh Down Souf.

An' I don' kheer, my hunny,
  Ef I gits wuck or not,
Fur de wadermillun's kumin',
  When de sun shines hot.

FELL FRUM GRACE.

I've bin brung befo' dis meetin',
    An' de truf I gwine to tell—
Yes, I took de jedge's chickens,
    An' sense den my min's a hell.
So, my brudders, I pleads guilty,
    An' I owns up lik' er man
Dat is kotched whil' doin' murder
    Wid de blood upon his han's.

Gwine to tell a straight tale 'bout it—
    Not a thing I gwine konseal,
'Cause my konshuns don' kondem me;
    De Lod he knows how bad I feel.
Ez I passed Jedge Johnson's manshun,
    Ez I'd of'en don' befo',
Dar I spied his hin-house open,
    'Dout no lock upon de do'.

'Weh Down Souf.

Brudders, won't y'all own t'wuz temptin'?
  So I kayed dem chickins off,
An' jes' only fur saf' keepin',
  Took an' hid 'um in de lof'.
All night long I thought erbout it—
  "Shell I tak' dem chickins back?"
But de ve'y nex' day wuz Krismus,—
  Is y'all 'sprised I jumped de track?

Forty years bin in good standin',
  Hoed my ro' in shade an' shine;
Nuther saint nor sinner suffud
  From no low-down ack ub min'.
But, ez yuthers don' befo' me,
  I jis' halted in de race,
An' de fus' thing dat I knowed un
  I had tumbled down frum grace.

Do' I makes a full confeshun,
  Yet I feel I 'zerbs yer raf,
But in mussy sphar er sinner
  Dat hez stumbled frum de paf;

'Weh Down Souf.

An' I makes dis 'umble promis'
   'Fore de chuch upon my knee,
Dat hereafter I shall try to
   Let my neighbors chickins be.

I jes' tol' de jedge erbout it—
   He had of'en gin me lif',—
What y'all reggin dat he tol' me?
   "Tak' dem fur my Krismus gif'."
I so glad I couldn't thank him,
   An' my eyes stretch wid surpris',
Den he sed dat I wuz hones'—
   Gin me dollah, too, besiz'.

Then up spoke the good old pastor:
   "Ez de Lord duz always keep
Larg' kumpashun fur de strayin',
   We forgibs dis erin' sheep.
Should Gabul serch dis congregashun
   Fur de chickins dat don' gone,
I'm mighty feard we'd all be lackin',
   So don' let us cast a stone."

'Weh Down Souf.

Then the chuch burst into singing
As they'd never sung before,
And the preacher told the sinner:
" Go in peace an' sin no mo'."

CHRISTMAS DREAMS.

As I sit to-night I'm dreaming,
While the moonlight's brightly beaming
And the stars keep watch above me,
For my heart is light and free.
Now a vision comes before me,
And a joy is stealing o'er me,
As in dreams I see my stocking
Hanging 'neath the mantle tree.

Now my mother comes before me,
And is lightly bending o'er me—
Looks to see if I am sleeping,
So that Santa Claus may come.
She stoops to kiss me fondly,
While things grow dim around me,
And I'm far away in dreamland,
While she softly leaves the room.

In the morning, quickly waking,
While my heart with joy is quaking,

'Weh Down Souf.

As I wonder if Old Santa
Could have coldly passed me by;
Oh! what happy, blissful feeling
To my raptured sight revealing,
As a world of Santa's goodies
Greet my eager, watching eye.

Now I wake—'twas only dreaming—
And the thoughts so blissful seeming
Pass away in gloomy shadows,
And the world seems dark and cold;
Mother's gone from earthly sorrow,
In the sweet and bright to-morrow
Where, an angel fair, she's watching
O'er the lambs of Heaven's fold.

In this world there still is grieving
I, her child, must be relieving,
While the pealing bells of Christmas,
Chiming on the evening air,
Bring sweet joy to hearts now breaking,
Help the downcast and forsaken,
Tell the bruised and the bleeding
That the world is still so fair.

"But when she had to turn erroun'
Fur sumpin' she furgits,
She meks a cross-mark on de groun'
An' turns erroun' an' spits."

SIGNS.

My Sarah Ann don' b'leve in signs,
    Sense she don' bin to skule;
She sez we folks ain't got no sense,
    An' almos' calls us fools.
Wid all de changes she don' made,
    One thing I know fur sho',
She don' bresh all de cobwebs down,
    But de horseshoe's ober de do'.

An 'tother day she start to chuch
    Wid all her fal-de-rals,
'Long Lucy Ann an' 'Rushy Jeems,
    An' lots er yuther gals;
But when she had to turn erroun'
    Fur sumpin' she furgits,
She meks a cross-mark on de groun'
    An' turns erroun' an' spits.

'Weh Down Souf.

An' when her nose begin to itch
    Huccum she stays at hom'?—
'Cause dat dar sign don' nebber fail—
    Somebody gwine ter kum;
But t'ain't no use ter tell me, do',
    Dar's sump'n in de min'
Ub ebry true-bon' cullud gal
    Dat meks her b'leve in signs.

I prides myself upon my wuck
    When I whitewash a fence—
De man dat won' be satisfied
    Mus' surt'ny lack fur sense;
But when dese sizly-sozly rains
    Kum fallin' to de groun'
An' wash aginst it long ernough,
    Dat whitewash mus' kum down.

So 'tiz wid ebry cullud chil',
    Do' it may be my own,
De skules kin nebber 'raderkate
    De thing dats in de bon'.—

'Weh Down Souf.

While folks is gittin' smart, ez sho'
    Ez whitewash made frum lime.
I gwine b'leve what de Bible sez
    Erbout signs ub de times.

THE OWL SONG.

(A song of the "Owl Club.")

Bird of the night! to thee,
Perched on the forest tree,
  Our song we raise;
Thy deeds we celebrate,
And thy great works narrate,
Thy fame we advocate,
  In notes of praise.

The turkey may be sweet,
And many birds you meet
  Are splendid "fowl"—
Not e'en the eagle bold,
Nor birds with plumage gold,
Nor song-birds young or old,
  Can touch thee, Owl!

46

'Weh Down Souf.

And whence comes thy great name,
Bird of the noble fame !
     Of being wise?
'Tis for thy silent tongue
That oft thy praise is sung,
And oft thy name is rung
     Up to the skies.

DE NIGGER'S GOT TO GO.

Dear Liza, I is bin down-town
   To Marster Charley's sto',
An' all de talk dis nigger hear
   Is, "Niggers got to go."
I 'fess it bodders my ol' head,
   An' I would lik' to kno',
What all we cullud folks is don',
   Dat now we'z got to go?

I hear dem say dat long ago
   To ol' Virginny's sho',
Dar kum a ship wid cullud folks,
   Sum twenty odd or mo';
Dey tells me dat dey hoed de corn,
   An' wuz good wuckers, sho',
Dey made Virginny like de rose—
   But now dey's got to go.

'Weh Down Souf.

Dat, when ol' Ginnel Washin'ton
   Did whip dem Red-koats so,
A nigger wuz de fus' to fall
   A-fightin' ub de fo';
Dat, in de late "unpleasunness"
   Dey watched at marster's do',
Proteckin' ub his lubin' ones,—
   But now dey's got to go.

I 'fess I lubs dis dear ol' place—
   'Twuz here we beried Jo';
An' little Liza married off,
   So menny years ago.
An' now wez feeble, an' our lim's
   A-gitting mighty slo'.
We'd hate to lebe de dear ol' place—
   But den, wez got to go.

I don't kno' much 'bout politicks,
   An' all dem things, yo' kno',
But de las' 'leckshun I jes' vote
   Ez de whi' folks tol' me to;

'Weh Down Souf.

Dey tole me vote fur Dimikrats,
   An' 'twould be better, 'do'
Sense now dey don' de leckshun win,
   Dey sez we'z got to go.

Dey sez de whi' folks mad 'long us,
   'Cause we kummin' up, yo' kno';
An' sum un us is gittin' rich,
   Wid do'-bells on de do';
An' got sum lawyers, doctors too,
   An' men like dat, fur sho'.
But den it kan't be jes' fur dis
   Dat we all got to go.

De Lord he made dis lubly lan'
   Fur white an' black folks too,
An' gin each man his roe to ten'—
   Den what we gwine to do?
We 'habes ouselbes an' 'specks de laws,
   But dey's peckin mo' an' mo'.
We ain't don' nuffin 't all to dem,
   Den huccum we mus' go?

'Weh Down Souf.

Fur ebry nashun on de glob'
   Dis seems to be a hom';
Dey welkums dem wid open arms,
   No matter whar dey frum;
But we, who here wuz bred an' borhn,
   Don't seem to hab no show;
We ho'ped to mek it what it is,
   But still we'z got to go.

It 'pears to me, my Liza, dear,
   We'z got a right to stay,
An' not a man on dis broad urf
   Gwine dribe dis nigger 'way.
But why kan't whi' folks lef us lon',
   An' weed dar side de ro';
An' what dey all time talkin' 'bout—
   " De nigger's got to go ? "

" 'Rastus," Liza sed, " trus' in God,
   He'll fix things here belo',
He don't hate us bekase we'z black—
   He made us all, yo' kno';

'Weh Down Souf.

He lubs us, ef we'z cullud folks,
   Ef de hart is white an' pure,
An' 'cepin' de Lord sez,—'Forward, march!'
   We'z not a-gwine to go.''

THE BABY SHOW.

Babies large, and babies small,
   And babies fat and fair;
The fond mammas and fond papas
   Had all the young ones there.

"'The paper man" just viewed the scene,
   And decided in a minute;
That the infant with the "kinky-top"
   Was certainly not "in it."

A few, though fat and chubby sprites,
   With mothers to defend them,
Because their colors "ran to dark,"
   Had nothing to commend them.

Perhaps to some this argues ill,
   And some no doubt are frightened;
But, to my mind, it demonstrates
   We are simply being *enlightened*.

DE LININ' UB DE HYMNS.

Dar's a mighty row in Zion, an' de debbil's gittin'
    high,

An' de saints don' beat de sinnuz, a-cussin on de
    sly.

What fur it am, you reggin? I'll tell you how it 'gin;

'Twuz 'bout a berry leetle thing — de linin' ub a
    hymn.

De young folks say 'tain't stylish to lin' 'um out
    no mo';

Dat dey's got edikashun, an' dey wants us all to
    know

Dey likes to hab dar singin'-books a-holin' fore dar
    eyes,

An' sing de hymns right straight along " to man-
    shuns in de skies."

Dat it am awful fogy to give 'um out by lin',

An' ef de ol' folks will kumplain 'cause dey is ol'
    an' blin',

'Weh Down Souf.

An' slabry's chain don' kep' dem back frum larnin'
    how to read—
Dat dey mus' take a corner seat, an' let de young
    folks lead.

We bin 'peatin' 'hine de pastor when he sez dat
    lubly prayhr,
'Cause sum un us don' kno' it, an' kin not say it
    squahr;
But now we mus' 'peat *wid* him, an ef we kan't
    keep time,
De gospil train will drap us off from follin' on
    behin'.

Well, p'raps dey's right, I kin not say; my lims is
    growin' ol',
But I likes to sing de dear ol' hymns, 'tiz music to
    my soul;
An' 'pears to me 'twont do much harm to gin 'um
    out by line,
Dat we ol' folks dat kin not read may foller 'long
    behin'.

'Weh Down Souf.

But few ub us am lef' here now dat bore de slabry
      chain,
We don' edikate our boys an' gals, an' would do
      de same again;
An Zion's all dat's lef' us now to cheer us wid its
      song—
Dey mought 'low us to sing wid dem, it kin not be
      fur long.

De sarmon's highfalutin', an' de chuch am mighty
      fin';
We trus' dat God still understan's ez in de days
      ub min',
When we, 'do' ignunt, po' an' mean, still wushuped
      wid de soul,
Whil' oft across our peaceful breas' de wabes ub
      trouble roll.

De ol'-time groans an' shouts an' moans am passin'
      out ub sight—
Edikashun changed all dat, an' we belebe it right,
We should serb God wid 'telligence; fur dis one
      thing I plead:
Jes' lebe a leetle place in chuch fur dem ez kin not
      read.

STICKIN' TO DE HOE.

Dar's mighty things a-gwine on,
   Sense de days when I wuz young,
An' folks don't do ez dey did once,
   Sense dese new times is kum;
De gals dey dresses pow'ful fin',
   An' all am fur a sho',
But de thing dat I'ze in favor ub
   Is stickin' to de hoe.

Larnin' is a blessed thing,
   An' good cloze berry fin',
But I likes to see de cullud gal
   Dat's been larnt how to 'ine';
Gimme de gal to wash an' scrub,
   An' keep things white an' clean,
An' kin den go in de kitchin
   An' cook de ham an' greens.

57

'Weh Down Souf.

I ain't got no edikashun,
　　But dis I kno' am true,
Dat raisin' gals too good to wuck
　　Ain't nebber gwine to do;
Dese boys dat look good 'nuf to eat,
　　But too good to saw de logs,
Am kay'n us ez fas' ez smoke,
　　To lan' us at de dogs.

I 'spose dat I'm ol' fashun',
　　But God made man to plow,
An' git his libbin by de sweat
　　Dat trickles down his brow.
While larnin' an' all dem things
　　Am mighty good fur sho',
De bes' way we kin make our pints
　　Is—stickin' to de hoe.

To fill de hed wid larnin'
　　Dat de fingers kan't express,
To dis poor ig'nunt brudder
　　Don't seem to be de bes';

58

'Weh Down Souf.

To git de edikashun
　An' larn to work ez well,
Seems to my 'umble judgment,
　De thing dat's gwine to tell.

MY CHILDHOOD'S HAPPY DAYS.

Many poets great and gifted, whom the Muse's
    touch has blessed,
Have sung in rhythmic measure, at the spirit's high
    behest,
Of the days of childish glory, free from sorrow and
    from pain,
When all was joy and pleasure—and wished them
    back again;
But, somehow, when my mind turns back to sing
    in joyous lays,
I remember great discomforts in my childhood's
    happy days.

Why, my earliest recollections are of pains and col-
    ics sore,
With the meanest kinds of medicines the grown
    folks down would pour—

'Weh Down Souf.

Ipecac and paregoric—and though I hard would
    kick,
They still would dose and physic, "'Cause the
    baby must be sick."
When I think of this, how can I sing a song in joy-
    ous lays,
And speak in tones of rapture of my childhood's
    happy days?

Off to school I then was started, and the simple
    rule of three
Was as hard as now quadratics or geometry's to
    me.
And then the awful thrashings with a paddle at the
    school,
And again at home with switches if I broke the
    simplest rule.
Oh! my life was one vast torment—so, of course,
    I'm bound to praise
The time that poets nickname "our childhood's
    happy days."

'Weh Down Souf.

On a cold December morning, when lying snug in
    bed,
I heard the sound, "You, Webster!" and I wished
    that I was dead.
I knew I had the fires to make, bring water, and
    cut wood;
And then, perhaps, I might have chance to get a
    bit of food,
When on to school I trotted. These were the
    pleasant ways
In which I spent that "festive time,"— my child-
    hood's happy days.

Father's breeches, cut to fit me, was, of course,
    the proper thing;
And nowhere did they touch me; my one "gallus"
    was a string;
I couldn't tell the front from back part; and my
    coat of navy blue
So variously was mended, it would match the rain-
    bow's hue.
'Twill do all right for rich white boys to sing these
    merry lays,
But the average little "Jap" fared tough in child-
    hood's happy days.

'Weh Down Souf.

I had a place back of my head the comb could
    never touch—

I'd jump three feet when tested. At last I cried
    so much,

Mother said that she would cut it. Oh, fate! to
    see me then.

My head was picked by dull shears, as if some tur-
    key hen

Had gotten in her cruel work; and the boys with
    jolly ways

Hallo'ed "buzzard!" when they saw me, "in
    childhood's happy days."

In the evening, holding horses, selling papers—
    "Evening News!"

To earn an honest penny for the folks at home to use.

Yet, of course, I had my pleasures—stealing sugar,
    playing ball,—

But I can not go in raptures o'er that season, after
    all.

And we repeat our childhood, and all life's sterner
    ways

Are mixed with rain and sunshine, as were child-
    hood's happy days.

'Weh Down Souf.

Still I find that life's a " hustle " from the cradle
    to the tomb,

With little beams of sunshine to lighten up the
    gloom.

If we can help a brother, and mix our cares with
    joys,

Old age will be as happy as the days when we were
    boys,

Till at last we sing in rapture heav'nly songs of
    love and praise,

When our bark is safely anchored,—there to spend
    our happiest days.

EXPOSITION ODE.

Read at the opening of the Negro Building, Atlanta, Ga.,
October 21st, 1895.

To-day we come to show the world what God for
    us hath wrought—
Here, where but thirty years ago we were as chat-
    tel bought;
He, painting us a darker hue, with hair more deep-
    ly curled,
Has blessed us with both brain and brawn, the
    conquerors of the world.

With grateful hearts we thank the men who gave to
    us the chance
To show the world our progress made, our useful-
    ness enhance.
Yet, 'twas our right, and not a man in justice
    could oppose,
For Negro hands made " Dixie " bloom and blos-
    som as the rose.

'Weh Down Souf.

We bring to-day just what we have, from school
    and shop and farm—
The products all of Negro brain, the fruit of his
    own arm.
Judged, not by heights that we have reached, but
    depths from whence we came,
There's not a Negro in the land need hang his head
    in shame.

We'll show the North their millions spent have not
    been spent in vain;
We'll show the South skilled laborers, who do not
    strike for gain;
We've left for aye our rude estate, to shape our
    lives by rule,
And banished Reconstruction's dream — "forty
    acres and a mule."

Our children here will come and view with pride
    this great display,
And babes unborn will bless us for the page we
    write to-day;

'Weh Down Souf.

We'll prove to all the Negro's worth, who here
    may wish to come,
To see what we black men have done to build up
    this our home.

We have a place in " Dixie Land;" our labor built
    its roads;
We cleared its forests, tilled its fields, and bore
    the heaviest loads;
Our blood was shed in its defense, dispute it ye
    who will,
For Attuck fell at Boston; Peter Salem, Bunker
    Hill.

And in those dark and bloody days, while fierce
    the battle rolled,
As North and South had gathered arms and called
    each other foes,
A soldier brave upon the field, a faithful slave at
    home,
He then disdained to think of shame to loved ones
    left alone.

But, as a faithful watch-dog stands and guards with
    jealous eye,
He cared for master's wife and child, and at the
    door would lie,
To shed his blood in their defense 'gainst traitors,
    thieves and knaves,
Although these masters went to fight to keep them
    helpless slaves.

What progress made? The answer's here for all
    who care to know.
We are not backward tending; but the best that
    we can show
Are men, who've made us what we are, the lead-
    ers in the van,
Our preachers, teachers, scholars—all an honor to
    the land.

A Brown, the prince of financiers; a Mitchell bold
    and true,
A Fortune, Gains and Washington, all men who
    dare and do;

'Weh Down Souf.

A Penn who gives us this display, and women good
  and fair,
We'll scale the heights by others reached, and place
  our banner there.

What tho' we've laggards in the ranks—all races
  have the same—
We'll opposition overcome, and march to wealth
  and fame;
With solid front for God and right, no en'my need
  assail,
For "right is right as God is God," and justice
  must prevail.

But slav'ry's rude and galling yoke has left on us
  its stain;
Divisions, petty jealousies and hate oft spoil our
  aim;
And struggling 'neath the damning yoke, we rise
  and kiss the rod,
And with an agonizing cry stretch forth our hands
  to God.

'Weh Down Souf.

The South's our home; 'tis here our eyes beheld
    life's morning dawn,
And here at evening's close we'll rest, our toils
    and conflicts done.
No politicians should divide relationships divine,
No arm should sever friendships formed in " Days
    of Auld Lang Syne."

Here tropic birds their matins sing, and sweet the
    streamlets flow,
And kindly nature gently smiles upon the vale be-
    low.
Shall we who made it what it is by sweat and pain
    and toil,
Be thought to be unworthy of a place upon its soil?

Here scented zephyrs fan the cheek, and heavenly
    music swells,
And God's own matchless finger paints the lovely
    hills and dells;
Here scented fragrance fills the air, and bright the
    flowers smile—
Shall ev'ry scene delight the view, and only man
    be vile?

'Weh Down Souf.

God is not dead, though justice sleeps, and right
    must conquer might.
The South's our common country, each must strive
    to do the right;
Too long we've looked outside ourselves to seek
    some guiding star;
We'll cease and " let our buckets down in places
    where we are."

With interests one and hopes the same, we'll look
    like hopeful youth,
To see the new sun dawning with its satellites of
    truth;
Disfranchisement, injustice and prejudices gone,
We'll both rejoice together at the coming of the
    dawn.

Filled with these expectations now, our hope takes
    fancy's wing;
But not alone as poet, but as prophet may we sing:
This scene will help its dawning—God grant we
    view its birth!
For " Dixie Land " is still to us the fairest spot
    on earth.

SKEETIN' ON DE ICE.

At a little country meeting, in a log house near
    the road,
The saints had duly gathered "fur de wushup ub
    de Lord,"
When "Bru Levi 'sen' de pulpit," cleared his
    throat, and then began:
"De 'spoundin' ub de scripshur, fur to cheer de
    speretu'l man."

I was teacher in the county, and was in duty bound
In attendance on the services, to help the breth-
    ren 'long.
Brother Levi was the pastor, and dispensed the
    gospel here,
As he *misunderstood* it at twenty-five a year.

The day was warm and sultry, sleep was getting in
    my eyes,
When this most unique sermon made them open
    with surprise:

'Weh Down Souf.

" My belubbed congregashun, I bin preachin'
    'bout de 'possles,
An' took my tex' whar Paul poked his 'pissle at
    de 'Fezhuns.

But to-day I gwine to tell yo' 'bout de chillun ub
    de Lord,
How dey crossed de ragin' waters at de spekin' ub
    de word.
I know y'all long bin won'drin' how de chillun
    crossed de sea;
'Tiz jes' ez plain ez kin be to er 'sper'enced man
    like me.

You see, 'twuz in de winter when de chillun dar
    wuz led,
An' de norf win' wuz a-blowin' strong ernuf to raise
    de dead.
Now, yo' see, de thing wuz easy, an' likewise ber-
    ry nice,
Fur all de chillun had to do wuz to skeet across on
    ice.

But when ol' Farro kum along wid dem big chayut
    wheels,
De ice jes' broke, an' all er dem fell in head ober
    heels.''
This was hard on my intelligence as teacher of the
    school,
And so I rose and said a word, although against
    the rule:

"Beg pardon, brother pastor, but geographies,
    you know,
Say this land is in the tropics, where can be no
    ice or snow.''
"I thanks yo', do' I does not like no 'sturbmence
    on dis topic;
But in dem days 'twon't no gogerfies, so, 'course
    dar won't no tropics.''

You can see I was dumbfounded; the brethren
    said, "Amen,''—
And thus he then concluded, ere I could speak again:
"When yo' gwine to cross de water, yo' better
    tak' advice,
An' 'cepin' de Lord is wid yo', don't skeet across
    on ice.''

"*Ol' Lijah wuz de bes' man; he'd cut de pijin-wing,*
An' crack his heels togedder keepin' time."

OL' VIRGINNY REEL.

Ez I set to-night I'm thinkin' ub de days now pas'
      an' gon',
  'Weh down in ol' Virginny 'mong de cohn;
Whar de sweet pertaters growin' an' de wadermil-
      lun smiles,
  Fur down de Souf in Dixie I wuz bom.
Dat lan' to me is dearer dan all on urf besiz;
  I feel de tear drops down my ol' cheeks steal
Ez I think ub al de pledjur in de dear ol' sunny
      lan',
  A-dancin' ub de ol' Virginny reel.

When de daily toil wuz ober in de quarters we
      would meet,
  An' sich anudder scufflin' dar would be
To git Miss Susan Johnsing, de Ca'line County
      belle,
  To dance de fus' set on de flo' wid me.

'Weh Down Souf.

We'd " Walk ol' John de Blin' Man," play " Hus-
      ko, Ladies Turn,"
   Would " Grine de Bottle " or de " Bobkin
      Steal "
But 'twon't no use a-talkin'; de fun would jes'
      begin
   When all would dance de ol' Virginny reel.

Ef you nebber seed de moshun, I will tell yo' how
      it goes;
   'Tiz a-bobbin' up an' down, a hop an' jump,
An' a-turnin' ebry lady ez yo' kum back down de
      line,
   Jes' like a bobtail moc'sin roun' de stump.
" Miss Liza Jane " is lubly, an' " Balmoral " is
      fin',
   An' " Wipe dem Di'mon' Winders " makes you
      feel;
But not " Bounce Aroun' My Sugar Lump," nor
      " Turnin' Good Ol' Man,"
   Ken 'gin to tetch de ol' Virginny reel.

'Weh Down Souf.

Dar's "Jinny Put de Kittle On," an' "Shoo!
    Miss Pijie, Shoo!"
  An' den "King William Wuz King George's Son,"
"Blin' Man Buff," an "Gimme Korner;" also
    "Walk de Lonesum Road,"
  Whar de pint wuz gittin' kisses—shorz yo' born;
But now dey 'fuse to play dem, an' kissin's out er
    style,
  'Cause now we folks is gittin' mighty high;
But den 'twuz free an' in'cent, 'dout a bit ub
    harm;
  'Twuz better'n doin' kissin' on de sly.

Ol' 'Lijah wuz de bes' man; he'd cut de pijin-wing,
  An' crack his heels togedder keepin' time;
His teef wuz like de tom'-stones, an' face like pos-
    sum fat,
  An' ebry knot wuz stickin' out behin'.
De gals wuz dressed in hom'spun, 'long wid dar
    brogan shoes,
  An' ef dar feet would tetch yo', yo' would feel,
'Do' de boys wore bed-tuck breeches, dese trifles
    wuz forgot,
  While 'joyin' ub de ol' Virginny reel.

'Weh Down Souf.

An' somehow ez I think agin ub bygone happy
    days,
  'Do' cares an' sorrows menny wuz our lot,
Dis lesson presses on me—an' forgib me when I
    say:
  Yo' should alway 'joy de blessin's dat yo' got.
An' den I sometimes wonder, ez I see y'all hop-
    pin' roun',
  Wid waltzes, polkas, dances toe an' heel,
Ef you really hab de pledjur, an' ez little ub de sin,
  Ez we in dancin' ol' Virginny reel.

A ROSE.

This rose of the garden is given to me,
And to double its value, 'twas given by thee;
Its lovely bright tints to my eyesight is borne,
Like the kiss of a fairy or blush of the morn.

How sweet is the fragrance that is wafted to me,
As the scent of the breeze from the isles of the sea.
It tells of the care of that Father above,
Who sends us the fragrance to show us His love.

Too soon must this scent-laden flower decay,
Its bright leaves will wither, its bloom die away;
But in mem'ry 'twill linger, the joy that it bore
Will live with me still tho' the flower's no more.

Fond hopes, too, must perish, its green leaves
    must die,
And sweet expectations all withered must lie;

'Weh Down Souf.

But He who has loved us and given His Son,
Sets the bow of His promise, and bids us hope on.

May our friendship ne'er perish, its strength ne'er
      decay,
But may it grow stronger and stronger each day,
And may the All-Father His love o'er us bend,
Till life is completed and heaven the end.

POMP'S CASE ARGUED.

Pomp stole dem breeches, an' 'lowed 'twon't sin,
'Cause he stole de breeches to be baptized in;
But I doubts dat, brudders; le's argify de case,
Fur we can't hab de young lams a-fallin' frum
      grace.

Ef er brudder is hongry, an' er chickin on de roos'
Sets a-temptin' ub de saints, why 'twon't no use
Fur de callin' ub er council; de case am plain,
De chickin wuz de sinner an' dezerbs all de blam'.

But breeches is dif'funt, an' stealin's mighty 'rong,
'Cause, yo' see, he moughter borro'd, sense his
      mem'ry ain' long;
An' furgittin' to return 'um, nobody could er say
Dat he stole dem breeches,—'tiz clear ez de day.

True, his moughter bin busted, an' de seat to'ed
      out—
Fur 'tiz kinder strainin', dis leadin' ub de shout;

But, den, he could er patched 'um, an' wid coat
      tails long
Hab cut a lubly figger 'dout doin' enny 'rong.

Maybe prid' wuz de kashun—dar de debbil tempts
      to sin,—
An' his bed-tick breeches won't good 'nuf fur him;
But I moves fur to 'sclude him, 'cause he nebber
      had to ought,
Ef he stole dem breeches, go an' git hisef caught.

WHEN YOU GITS A RABBIT FOOT.

Yo' kin always hab a dollah,
　　When yo' gits a rabbit-foot;
'Cause de luck is bound to follah,
　　When yo' gits a rabbit-foot.
You may not want to tak' it,
　　But 'tiz so, shorz yo' born,
No matter how yo' mak' it,
　　I'm always gwine to own
　　　　A good ol' rabbit-foot.

All yer trubbles seem to lebe yo',
　　When yo' gits a rabbit-foot;
Nobody kin decebe yo',
　　When yo' gits a rabbit-foot.
Jes' always git a lef' foot,
　　Don't nebber git de right;
Ketch de rabbit in a grabeyard,
　　'Bout de middle ub de night—
　　　　Dat's de kind ub rabbit-foot.

'Weh Down Souf.

Git de lef' foot dat's behin',
  Dat's de lucky rabbit-foot;
An' ef de rabbit's blin',
  Dat's a sho' rabbit-foot;
'Tiz better'n habin' munny,
  'Cause dat may git away,
But wid de proper rabbit-foot
  Yer luck is dar to stay.
      Jes' git a rabbit-foot.

You'll git offis 'dout votin',
  Ef yo' got a rabbit-foot;
All dese rich folks is a-totin'
  One dese same rabbit-foots.
Sum dese edikated people
  Dat's a-laffin' so at me,
Ef you'd look into dar pockets,
  I lay ennything you'd see
      Dey's got a rabbit-foot.

MAT.

In the swamp by a black gum, in a little log hut
        Lived Mat,
The toughest little fellow, in tatters and rags
        At that;
"A reg'lar good-for-nothing," the neighbors all
        vowed.
He would rob a hen's nest; not a melon he allowed
To remain in the patch—yet we, for all that
        Liked Mat.

With his tatters all flying and a crownless hat
        Came Mat
'Cross the hill by the corn-field and "sweet-tater"
        patch,
        And that
Was a sign that the "taters" and corn had disap-
        peared,
For when Mat was about, why everybody feared;
But, then, when you saw him your sorrow changed
        that
        For Mat.

'Weh Down Souf.

For ten or eleven little brothers and sisters
> Had Mat,

And his poor mother labored to feed and to clothe
> them
>> At that;

And work in the country, when you wash the whole
> day,

And receive but a quarter is mighty poor pay,—

No wonder he was ragged, and would steal at that,
> Poor Mat!

Yet, the world often wonders, as it speeds on its
> way,
>> At the Mats,

Who are reared in ignorance, the world's "good-
> for-nothings;"
>> But for that,

How many called better, who have ne'er felt the
> smart

Of poverty's nettle can boast of a heart

As free from guile and as tender as that
> Of Mat.

DE CHANA CUP.

Our church had a meeting, where the brethren
    gathered
  To transact the business they had for the Lord,
To turn out the lambs who had strayed from the
    sheep-fold,
    And to take in repentants in accord with his
    word.
The axe had been falling with impartiality
  On drunkards and policy-players of old,
On sisters who'd fallen from pathways of virtue,
    And all who had wandered like sheep from the
    fold.

At last came a sister whose skirts were all muddy,
  With drabbling in sin all the days of her youth,
Had been caught and excluded 'mid tears of the
    brethren,
  But now would return to the pathway of truth.

'Weh Down Souf.

"I am truly repentant, the Lord has forgiven;
  Since last month, when excluded, I've prayed
    night and day.
Will you, brethren, forgive and restore me to fel-
    lowship,
  And, with Jesus to guide, I'll no more go
    astray?"

"Bless the Lord!" said the brethren; "Amen!"
    said the sisters,
  "Thank God, she's returning; I move—take
    her in."
The motion was carried with great hallelujahs
  For the sister restored from the by-ways of
    sin.
Brother Slaughter waxed warm, and spoke of the
    prodigal,
  And the rejoicing in heaven ɔ'er sinners re-
    turned:
"Ef yo' fall, don't yo' woller, yo' kin tell a true
    Christyun,
  Fur down in de heart speretu'l oil will burn."

'Weh Down Souf.

" De sister am good ez befo', ef not better,
  Fur dear is de lam's when returned to de fol',
Ef yuz gwine ter sin, jes' be sho' yo' don't woller,
  An' yo' sho' ub de glory ez a pijin his hole."
Up spoke Brother Van: " My brudder, hol' on,
    dar!
  Youz ressin de skripshur, an' leadin' us wrong.
'Taint better to wander den keep de straight paf-
    way,
  An' de Lord lubs de young lam's dat keep right
    along."

" I once had a chana cup I sot right much sto' by,
  One day bein' keerless, I drapped on de flo'.
I patched it wid glu', sah, an' do' it held water,
  It nebber did ring like it did befo'.
Yo' may dribe in a nail right in dis here pos' here,
  Den draw out de nail, but *de hole is still dar;*
Yo' may bu'n your fhar arm, an' heal up de bu'n,
    sah,
  But de schar gwy tell on you wharebber you
    ar'."

89

"True, de prodigal son got sum cloze an' sum
vittles,
But long he'd been starbin' wid nuthin' to wahr,
While de boy dat staid hom' got de bes' ub de
pickins,
Wid lots er fin' raimen', an' plenty to sphar.
Yo' wimmen who stray from de pafway ub virtue,
May be 'sto'ed to de chuch an' yer sins plas-
tered o'er;
But like bells widout clappers mus' always remain,
sah,
An' dey nebber kin ring like dey did befo'."

I CAN TRUST.

I can not see why trials come,
  And sorrows follow thick and fast;
I can not fathom His designs,
  Nor why my pleasures can not last,
Nor why my hopes so soon are dust;
      But I can trust.

When darkest clouds my sky o'erhang,
  And sadness seems to fill the land,
I calmly trust his promise sweet,
  And cling to His ne'er-failing hand,
And in life's darkest hour I'll just
      Look up and trust.

I know my life with Him is safe,
  And all things still must work for good
To those who love and serve our God,
  And lean on Him as children should.
'Though hopes decay and turn to dust,
      I still will trust.

OLD NORMAL:

Read before the Alumni Association of the Richmond High Normal School.

Old Time with his sickle, in swift onward play,

For once has turned backward; we're children to-
day,

And the world with its conflicts, its battles and
strife,

Is forgotten in pleasures and mem'ries of life.

These girls with their puffs, bangs and frizzes ga-
lore,

Are again in short dresses, with white pinafore;

While the men, with stiff collars and high beaver
hat,

Are boys in short breeches, and patched ones at
that.

As I'm standing here reading, I'm quaking with
fear,

For I think 'tis Miss Stratton whose footsteps I
hear;

'Weh Down Souf.

Or dear Mr. Manly, or sainted Miss Knowles,
Comes tripping behind me, just ready to scold.

"Please, Webster, sit down there!" I fancy she
     calls,
While Miss Manly, Miss Hadley, Miss Patterson—all
Come trooping before me.   But one thing I know:
I can step by Miss Bass, she's so awfully slow.

My name is still cut on the seat by the door—
I'm trying to cut higher than in days of yore;
Yet I wonder if fame can give me the joy
I found at old Normal when I was a boy.

On the green field of life we're playing some game;
Our base-ball and foot-ball we're playing the same.
If we fail in our kicking, let us strive all the more,
The world kicks much harder than Normal of yore.

Some now make a home-run, and multitudes shout;
While some strike a grounder, and others strike out.
Tho' fallen and beaten, we still must be men,
And try it to-morrow to win if we can.

'Weh Down Souf.

Our girls of old Normal are still jumping rope—
But don't let it trip you and get your neck broke,
For few, like old Normal, will help us, alas!
When once we have fallen from virtue's straight
      path.

But well we remember no boyhood could last;
The world called for men, and we went to our task;
Some won and some failed, but in heart we are
      one,
I trust just as true as the day we begun.

Some fellows are lawyers, and sending to jail
Their poor fellow-creatures, nor getting them bail;
While others are doctors, and curing life's ills—
At least, if not curing, are sending in bills.

Some now are professors and teachers in schools,
And thrashing young urchins for breaking the rules;
Some maidens, some matrons, and some fond
      mammas,
With children to try them and break all their laws.

'Weh Down Souf.

What though they are climbing the ladder of fame;
They are Ben, Dan or Bowler—Hayes, Johnston or
    James;
Though clouded with care, and in dignified dress,
They are Sallie and Julia, Rose, Anna and Bess.

Some fellows are down now who then strove for
    fame—
Maybe gone to the bad;—they are ours the same;
Let's throw them a life-line who're sinking in crime,
And allure them to virtue for dear "Auld Lang
    Syne."

But some fail to answer at call of the roll;
Our eyes fill with tears—they are missed from the
    fold;
In glory we'll greet them when battle is done;
Pat, Walter and others will meet us,—at home.

Let's recount our battles, take courage and aim
To help on each other to honor and fame;
Nor suffer our banner to trail in the dust,
Or the bright sword of honor in scabbard to rust.

'Weh Down Souf.

We think of our sorrows, we think of our joys,
And in this reunion are again girls and boys;
Old Time can not dampen our spirits so gay,
We'll laugh at his efforts,—we're children to-day.

By this hallowed Elysium our tent is now spread,
But soon to new duties—new paths we must tread;
The world calls for heroes; our race calls for men,
Unselfish and true to our duty as then.

GINGER SNAPS AND CIDER.

Again the Christmas time is here,
    With joy in fullest measure,
And every fellow, great and small,
    Is looking out for pleasure.
To me the days no brighter seem,
    Although my vision's wider,
Than when I was a country lad,
    With ginger snaps and cider.

And when 'twas near " hog-killin' time,"
    The world seemed to me bigger,
For Christmas then was on the way,
    When I could cut a " figger;"
Most homely were the joys we had—
    " Molasses stews " and " parties "—
But innocent the joy they gave,
    With fun both pure and hearty.

97

'Weh Down Souf.

Long past is now this simple joy,
  But, with the Christmas season,
Do I feel just as happy now,
  And with as good a reason?
I wonder if my heart's as free
  Now since my vision's wider,
As in those bygone Christmas days
  Of ginger snaps and cider?

Am I now deaf to sorrow's cry,
  Do I pass the poor unheeding?
Do I truly wish for them the joy
  For which their hearts are pleading?
Do I delight to bring a smile,
  And hearts cast down to brighten,
And sympathize with others' woes,
  And help their lots to brighten?

As came the "God-Man" from above
  To Bethl'hem's lowly manger,
To seek and save the wand'ring sheep,
  The homeless and the stranger;

'Weh Down Souf.

So be it ours some heart to cheer,
  As comes this time of pleasure,
And fill the cup of lonely ones
  With joy in fullest measure.

Some sit to-day in gilded halls,
  Secure from seeming troubles,
While others, with a single crust,
  Are shiv'ring in their hovels.
We wonder oft why this is true—
  But life, at best, is fleeting,
And oh, what recompense will come,
  With heaven's eternal meeting.

I sometimes think we're growing up
  To be a wondrous people,
But yet, I fear, in building we're
  Commencing with the steeple.
Without a basis broad and deep,
  With virtue its foundation,
And truth and right as corner-stones,
  We can not build a nation.

'Weh Down Souf.

On social hops and fancy balls
   Society now fattens,
But yet I find oft little souls
   May dwell 'neath silks and satins;
Hypocrisy, deceit and lies
   May mean our scope is wider,
But give me honest truth and love,
   With ginger snaps and cider.

I WONDER HOW THIS IS.

I'm not a bad fellow, but just " kinder midlin,"
  Not a devil incarnate, nor saint dressed in white;
But " 'bout half-and-half," with a sprinklin' of
    devil,
  And enough of the angel to keep me near right.

Yet often I wander; my feet get entangled,
  'Mid briers and quicksands too often I stray,
And anxious I ask can I reach the pathway,
  As sinful and crooked I oft lose my way.

Once I went to a funeral; the chap was a " tough
    one,"
  A gambler, a drunkard, he cheated and lied,
A deeply-dyed rascal, but gave big donations;
  So the preacher just fixed him all right when he
    died.

'Weh Down Souf.

I went to the graveyard and looked on the tomb-
    stones—
    What lovely inscriptions! all praising the dead;
Every one there was good, every one had reached
    heaven—
    I wondered where all the bad fellows were laid.

And thus says the world; if you've friends or have
    money
    You are certain of heaven, your sins plastered
    o'er;
But the poor, seedy devils who have empty pockets,
    Nobody knows if they're in heaven or no.

Perhaps this is right, and maybe up yonder
    The wonder will be, not that we were bad,
But as good as we have been, 'mid all of the weak-
    ness,
    And all the temptations that each must have had.

But we'll find lots of folks we thought were in heaven
    Have missed it; while others, assigned down be-
    low,
Are exalted, for there full justice is given;
    By the heart God judges the rich and the poor.

"'Scuze me, mistis, but dar's sumfin'
De matter wid dem strings."

MISS LIZA'S BANJER.

Hi! Miss Liza's got er banjer;
   Lemme see it, ef yo' please!
Now don' dat thing look pooty,
   A-layin' 'cross yer kneeze,
Wid all dem lubly ribbins,
   An' silber trimmin's roun'.
Now, mistis, please jes' tetch it,
   To lemme hear de soun'.

'Scuze me, mistis, but dar's sumfin'
   De matter wid dem strings;
I notis it don' zackly
   Gib de proper kinder ring;
An' den de way yo' hol' it
   Ain't lik' yo' orter do.
Now, mistis, won't yo' lemme
   Jes' try a chune fur yo'?

'Weh Down Souf.

Now lis'n to de diffunce;
   I'se got the thing in chune,
An' de music's lik' de breezes
   Dat fills de air in June.
Fur a banjer's lik' a 'ooman—
   Ef she's chuned de proper pitch,
She'll gib yo' out de music
   Dat's sof', melojus, rich.

But when yo' fail to chune her,
   Or to strike de proper string,
Yo' kin no more git de music,
   Den mek' a kat-bird sing.
An' 'taint always de fixin's
   Dat makes a 'ooman bes',
But de kind ub wood she's made un
   Is de thing to stan' de tes'.

I s'pose yer plays yer music
   Jes' lik' yo' hab it wrote,
Or—what is dat yo' call it—
   A-playin' by de note?

'Weh Down Souf.

Yo' kin fill yer head wid music
 Ez full ez it kin hol',
But yo' nebber gwine ter play it
 'Tell yo' gits it in yer soul.

T'ain't de proper notes dat makes yo'
 Feel lik' yo' wants to cry,
But de soul dat's in de music
 Dat lif's yo' up on high;
An' 'taint always de larnin',
 'Do' a splendid thing, I kno',
Dat lif's de low an' 'umble
 To higher things belo'.

Keep larnin', den, Miss Liza,
 An' when yo' wants ter know
Ef yo' kin play de banjer,
 Jes' kum to Uncle Joe;
Jes' fill yer head wid music,
 Ez full ez it kin hol'
But de music from de banjer
 Must fust be in de soul.

HOPE.

When evening shades, the night's fair warning,
   Doth gild the spires with the last lingering ray,
The sun's last tint is hope's bright dawning;
    The gloom will pass, the night shades fade away.
        Bright hope gives warning
        Of daylight's dawning,
When gloom is past, night's darkness chased away.

When sorrow, care and pain unceasing,
   Beset our pathway and our souls appall,
We still can trust that love unceasing
    That gilds the stars, yet marks the sparrow's fall.
        That love imploring,
        Our trust enduring,
Shall pierce the gloom by faith in Him, our All.

When death's dark night its shadows gathers,
   Hope brightly beams and sheds her cheering ray;
Whate'er betide, we trust our Father,
    Who clothes the fields with flowers in bright array.
        Through ages winging,
        His praises singing,
New life shall dawn with Heaven's eternal day.

DE BAPTIS' CHUCH.

I b'leves in 'lijun;
  An' I 'joys it, too,
'Cause I bin born, hunny,
  Right thu an' thu;
An' I bin dug up
  By de gospel plow,
An' I'm jes' sho' fur glory
  Ez I wuz dar now.

But, somehow or ruther,
  'Do' I kan't tell why,
Ef I wants to feel happy,
  Like I gwine fur to fly;
An' feel ef I died,
  I wouldn't kheer much—
I mus' 'ten' dem meetin's
  At de Baptis' chuch.

'Weh Down Souf.

De Mefdis' good,
   An' de Cammelites, too,
But it takes an' ol' Baptis'
   To sing 'um right thu;
An' I don' b'leve de sinner
   Ebber bin born,
Dat kin stan' out 'gainst
   A Baptis' mourn.

'Cause when ol' Lige
   Git his han' to his jaw,
An' 'gins fur to whoop 'um,
   An' snort an' rar,
De stoutest ol' sinner
   Is boun' fur to fall,
'Cause he can't stan' 'ginst
   Dat Baptis' call.

Maybe sprinklin's good,
   An' porin's right,
But berry me deep
   Down out er sight;

'Weh Down Souf.

"I'm Baptis' bred,
  An' Baptis' born,
An' when I'm ded
  Dar's a Baptis' gone."

I'm jes' a-libbin'
  De bes' I know,
An' tryin' to be hones',
  Whil' I'se here below;
'Cause dis I knows,
  Dat I done bin "born,"
An' I keeps on tootin'
  De Baptis' horn.

I don' know much
  'Bout doctrin's here,
An' de diffunt 'lijuns,
  An' I don' kheer;
Ef Gawd Ermighty ax me,
  I won't say much,
But tell Him I 'longed
  To de Baptis' chuch.

PAYIN' FUR DE HYDIN.

"Kum up here an' git salvashun,
'Tis fur eb'ry trib' an' nashun;
Kum all yo' pizin sinnuz,
Salvashun now is free;
Jes' step up to de fountin,
While de water is a-runnin';
Ef yo' wanter go to glory,
Jes' foller arter me."

"Now it ain't no use er talkin',
Fur de sperit is er walkin';
'Do' your sins is lik er mountin,
Jes' ez big ez big kin be,
Jes' a drop er dis huh water,
Ef you tak' it ez yo' orter,
Will make y'all brazin' sinnuz
Almos' jes' ez good ez me."

'Weh Down Souf.

The sermon soon was ended,
And the brethren said 'twas splendid,
And the sisters felt so happy,
That they scarcely touched the ground.
Then the deacon, old but sprightly,
Began to step up lightly,
To gather in the pennies,
As he passed the basket 'round.

" I dejecks," said Brother Peter,
A new converted "creeter,"
" Fur de pastor said salvashun,
Like de water huh wuz free."
" By dem words I is abidin',
But yo' mus' pay fur de hydin,"
Said the pastor, "an' yo' understan's,
De hydin huh is me."

OL' MISTIS.

Oh, de times is fas' a-changin',
　　Ez de years ar' rollin' on,
An' de days seem mighty lonesum',
　　Sense de good ol' times is gon'.
While I'm 'joycin' in my freedum,
　　Nor wish fur slab'ry days,
Yit it warms my heart to 'member
　　Sum good ol'-fashun ways.

De pledjur ub de harves'
　　De huntin' ub de coon,
'Weh down in de low groun',
　　By de shinin' ub de moon;
De dancin' in de cabin—
　　An' didn't we hab de fun,
While de banjer wuz a-twangin',
　　When de daily wuck wuz don'.

112

'Weh Down Souf.

Ub all de plezzun mem'riz,
    Dar's one dat fills my heart,
'Tiz de thought ub dear ol' Mistis,
    An' 'twill nebber frum me part.
No matter what de trubble
    De Lord wuz pleased to sen',
We had jes' to tell ol' Mistis,
    She would alwa's be a fren'.

Ef de oberseer 'buze us,
    An' frum de lash we'd run,
An' weery, col', an' starvin',
    Afeard to kum back hom',
Jes' git word to ol' Mistis,
    She'd smoov de trubble o'er,
An' back we'd kum a sneakin',
    An' hear ub it no mo'.

When sickness, kheer an' sorrow
    Gib nights ub akin' pain,
An' tears frum werry eyelids
    Kum pou'in' down like rain;

'Weh Down Souf.

Racked wid pains an' scotched wid febers,
   Wid lim's a-growin' col',
She had lin'ments fur de body,
   An' de Bible fur de soul.

An' when de 'partin' speerit
   Would fly to yuther lan's,
She'd gently clos' de eyelids
   Wid tender, reb'rent han's,
An' wid words ub consolation
   Would pint de heart abov',
To whar dar is no shadders—
   De heb'ny lan' ub lov'.

When de ebenin' sun wuz settin',
   On a Sunday arternoon,
We'd gether in de great house,
   An' jine her in a chune;
Den' she'd read de fam'ly Bible,
   An' lif' her soul in prayhr,
Tell I eenmos' see de angels,
   An' 'majin I wuz dar.

'Weh Down Souf.

All I knows erbout de 'lijun,
   I wuz teeched besize her knee,
All erbout de blessid Sabyur,
   Who died fur eben me;
An' when I gits to glory—
   It kan't be long, I kno'—
I specks to meet ol' Mistis
   On de bright an' happy sho'.

IS DAR WADERMILLUNS ON HIGH?

Dey tells erbout heben, an' de streets ub gol',
  An' de harp dat I'll play bime-by;
But de thing dat puzzles me mo' an' mo',
  Shell I eat wadermilluns on high?

Dey tells ub de robe, an' de starry crown,
  An' de ribber dat glides 'long by;
Ub de tree ub life, an' twelve kinder frut,
  But nuthin' 'bout milluns on high.

Dey sez dat de puh an' de good is blest
  Wid manshunz in de bright sky;
But nobody tells dis chile ub grace
  Dat he'll eat wadermilluns on high.

Dey sez dat my tears will be wiped away,
  No sorrer nor sighin' kum nigh;
But I think I'd cry tell my eyes bus' out,
  Could I git no milluns on high.

'Weh Down Souf.

Dey tells ub hunny an' milk an' things
   Dat de saints gwy git bime-by;
Den huccum dey kan't hab a wadermillun patch
   In de lubly green fiel's on high?

But in dat book what tells erbout heb'n
   Dey couldn't put all ef dey try,
An' de parts dats nebber bin writ, I think,
   Tells ub big wadermilluns on high.

COOKIN' BY DE OL'-TIME FIRE-PLACE.

I'be heard ub lots ub cookin' by de cooks dey say
  is fin',
 Dat fixes up dar eatin's by de books;
But wid all dar fancy dishes, dat may suit de high-
  est min',
 Dey kan't kum up to dese ol'-fashun cooks.

An' 'dough dey hab dar ranges, an' eb'ry thing in
  style,
 An' sumtimes, maybe, dey kin hit de tas'e;
But when it kums to cookin' dat kin beat dem all
  de whil',
 Git A'n' Dinah, an' de ol'-time fire-place.

She nebber had no lamin', but it kum jes' nat'yul
  so,
 She seemed to be cut out to suit de place;
An' Marster he wuz happy, howebber things would
  go,
 Wid A'n' Dinah at the ol'-time fire-place.

'Weh Down Souf.

She could bake de bes' ol' flab-jacks dat ebber
      yo' behol',
  Dat would mak' yer mouf jes' water all de while;
An' de way she'd roas' a possum, an' tak' him up
      right whole,
  Would mak' de baby in de cradle smile.

She could cook a sweet pertater 'tell 'twuz mealy
      to de mouf,
  An' bake a corn-cake to de proper brown;
Stew a ol' hare in de fashun yo' kin only fin' down
      Souf,
  An' tell when de pot don' bilin' by de soun'.

An' how she'd bake de ash-cake between de collud
      leaves!
  I couldn't begin to tell yo' ef I'd try;
But she wuz fines' in de county, I really do believe,
  When she'd tackle ol' Virginny pun'kin pie.

An' I kno' I could die happy, do' my pledjurs here
      am few,
  Ef befo' I finished up dis urfly race,
I could git a meal ub vittles, jes' like I used to do,
  When A'n' Dinah used de ol'-time fire-place.

UNCLE 'RASTUS AND THE WHISKEY QUESTION.

I don' hear dem rebolushuns 'bout whiskey en all
    dat,
But yo' ain't gwy nebber pas' 'um, I tells yo' dat
    right flat;
Don't let y'alls smartnis fool yo', en try to do too
    much,
'Cause yo' jes' gwy bring 'bout 'sturbance, en yo'
    tryin' to bus' dis chuch.

Y'all know dat whiskey bin here long ' fore we wuz
    born,
En t'ain't nebber trubbled nothin'——better let wel
    'nuf 'lone;
'Size, Paul don' tole you take it, jes' fur de stom-
    ach's sake,
We cert'ny gwy bay de scripshur, den what y'all
    speck to make?

'Weh Down Souf.

I hear y'all kote dat scripshur, " Ef eatin' meat
    'fen, don't eat."
But Paul won't talkin' 'bout whiskey, 'cause he
    pint'ly menshuns meat;
Dat drunkards khant reach Heben, de guard won't
    let 'um in,
But dat don't mean wid whiskey, but folks dat's
    drunk in sin.

" Look not on de wine cup," is what de Word tells
    me,
Well, don't dat mean to drink it?   'Tis plain ez
    plain ken be.
But we 'cided 'fore we kum here to vote dat
    moshun down,
'Cause we argued it at meetin's we had all ober
    town.

In kos we'z pozed to dancin' en all dem no-harm
    sins,
An' will turn 'um out like lightnin' ef tiz dem upper
    tens;
But all sich things ez drinkin', playin' policy en
    such,
Am far too triflin' matters to fotch befo' dis chuch.

NIGHT ON DE OL' PLANTASHUN.

Upon de ol' plantashun, jes' erbout de crack ub day,
    You could lis'en fur de oberseer's horn;
An' by sunrise we wuz movin', fur we had to git
      away,
    An' do an hones' day's wuck shorze yo' bo'n.
But when de shadders gethered, an' we had done
      our turn,
    We'd put away de shuvel an' de hoe,
Fur ol' marster never bothered, ef he knowed our
      wuck wuz done,
    Ef we den injoyed de fiddle an' de bow.

Sumtimes our wives an' chillun wuz on de 'jinin'
      farm,
    Maybe ten or 'leben miles or mo' away;
We'd walk it 'dout no trouble, nor did it don' us
      harm,
    An' be fresh an' ready fur de wuck nex' day.

'Weh Down Souf.

We could dodge de patterrollers ef we didn't hab
    a pass—
  Dat kind ub thing wuz only fun fur us—
An' 'stid ub us kumplainin', we 'joyed it to de las',
  An' wuz thankful to de Lord it won't no wuss.

Some would gether in de cabin, or in de corn-
    house, whar,
  Wid tubs an' pots an' kittles settin' roun',
Dey would rassle wid de Father in strong an'
    earnes' prayhr,
  Whil' de water in de vessels ketched de soun'.
'Cause 'do' we mout be sinnuz, an' wander frum
    de fol',
  Our 'zires wuz always right ez dey could be,
An' our 'pendunce in de Bible, whar ub de lan'
    we'z tol',
  Whar servunts frum de marster is set free.

Maybe ignunce made us happy when de marster
    treat us fair,
  An' unkumplainin' when we found him mean;
An' days ub toil an' trouble cheered by nights so
    free from care,
  On de ol' plantashun, now jes' like a dream.

'Weh Down Souf.

An' when ol' Death shall take us, whar night kin
    kum no mo',
  An' we meet in Heben above, to nebber roam,
We'll talk up dar togedder, wid loved ones gon'
    befo',
  Ub de nights in de ol' plantashun hom'.

AUNT CHLOE'S LULLABY.

Hesh! my baby; stop yer fuss,
I's 'fraid yuz gittin wuss an' wuss;
Doncher cry, an' I gwy mek'
Mammy's baby 'lasses cake.
Hesh! my lubly baby chil',
I gwy rock yo' all de whil';
Nuffin gwyne to ketch yo' now,
'Cause yer mammy's watchin' yo'.
Sleep! my little baby, sleep!
  Mammy's baby, Lou!

How dem dogs do bark to-night!
Better shet yer eyes up tight;
Dey kan't hab dis baby dear;
Mammy's watchin', doncher fear.
Hear dem owls a-hootin' so?
Dey shan't ketch dis baby, do'.
Jes' like mistis lub her chil',
Mammy lubs dis baby too.

'Weh Down Souf.

Sleep! my little baby, sleep!
    Mammy's baby, Lou!

Mammy's baby, black an' sweet,
Jes' like candy dat you eat,
Mammy lay yo' in dis bed,
While she mek de whi' folk's bread.
Angels dey gwy look below,
Watch dis baby sleepin' so.
Go to sleep, my hunny, now,
Ain't yer mammy watchin' yo'?
Sleep! my little baby, sleep!
    Mammy's baby, Lou.

GOOD NIGHT!

Good-night! The day is done,
And evening shadows softly fall—
    Good-night!
The night bird's gently cooing to its mate,
And slowly now the silv'ry moonbeams
Deck the evening sky with their pale rays,—
    Good-night! good-night!

Good-night! The day was long,
And weary feet now gladly say,
    Good-night!
Forgot is toil as gentle sleep,
The "sweet restorer," softly steals
And fills our eyes. To all we say,
    "Good-night! good-night!"

Good-night! Earth's day must close,
And Death's cold summons make us say,
    "Good-night!"

'Weh Down Souf.

The pain be past of life's rude days,
Our feet press hard on Jordan's brink,
And then to realms of blissful dreams—
    Good-night! good-night!

Good-night! We fondly hope
For us that brighter day will dawn.
    Good-night!
Oh! may we live in loving trust
That heaven's gate may open wide,
When earth's last scenes fade from our view.
    Good-night! good-night!

APPENDIX.

INTRODUCTION TO AUTHOR'S FIRST VOLUME OF POEMS.*

This volume of poems from the pen of a mind en.
dowed of God with rich fancy, which has been fertil-
ized by liberal culture, patient industry, and that
tact which makes most of opportunities, is presented
to the public as an illustration of the dialect or patois
of a part of the Negro race whose ancestry was
nearer Africa than the class represented in age and
opportunity by the writer of them.

These poems are tradition and history in dialect or
patois. They show the power, continuity and tenac-
ity of race under circumstances the most adverse and
the most untoward, as to its preservation of type and
language, the outgrowth of a condition the race was
powerless to relieve itself from, and which unconsciously stamped itself upon the people over thousands of miles of territory of a race foreign to the
Negro race.

Much that is best in the American Negro is tradi-
tional; all that is worst is historical, and not of his
writing.

In these poems the author has faithfully preserved

---

* The majority of tne poems in Mr. Davis's first book, "Idle
Moments," are republished in this book.—THE PUBLISHERS.

129

the dialect and something of the folk-lore of the Negro-American. The writer was born and reared in his loved Virginia. He came upon the scene just as the clouds and mists were rolling away. This nearness to slavery, this environment throughout his useful life as student and educator, makes these poems the more to be admired as a "counterfeit presentment," not alone of how the Southern Negro talked in days of slavery but of how the Southern whites talked, of how all the people, in the rural parts of the South talk now.

A peculiarly noticeable and interesting fact as to the physical strength of the Negro race type, all may see in the colored people, though the stream of Negro blood be so shallow as to be discernable only in the octoroon; yet the Negro is stamped indelibly in this class, in features, in hair or in some prominent race peculiarity. So also is the strength of impression made upon the English language of America as marked and distinctive in the dialect of all the people of the South Atlantic and the South and Southwestern States, without distinction of race.

There is no purpose to do Africa and our ancestry the injustice of implying that the language of the plantation is an African language, or an African provincialism, any more than to say that the plantation patois is English.

The great majority of Negroes brought from Africa into the colonies and later into the States of the United States, were, judged by appearances, of an inferior type from most of the races of that region, and in the main were Congo Africans, and brought with them their maternal language, the Congo, be-

Appendix.

tween which and the language of Europe there exists
the greatest dissimilarity. Those not natives to the
Congo region, were from the interior and coast
tribes. Now all the original immigrants were, by
the system of traffic peculiar to American slavery,
scattered throughout the colonies and the States.

The effect of this separation upon their language
was plainly shown in their adherence to the accentuation of it, to the peculiarity of pronunciation of English words, a peculiarity inseparable from the bent
of their mother tongue, their African languages.

These peculiarities of speech were transmitted from
father to son in an unbroken line of centuries. Yet
so strong have been the cords and chains of language, where the race has been most numerous, that
the training of the schools has not been able to break
the hold of paternal speech, an admixture of African
accentuation grafted upon European languages — as
spoken in the United States.

One illustration will serve to make plain the fact
now dwelt upon. There appears to be no race of
Europeans, the English excepted, who pronounce the
Greek *theta*, as the ancient Greeks did. There is no
African who has reached his majority in Africa
whom I have heard of, who can pronounce as did
the Greeks and Anglo-Saxons, *theta*, *th.*

In this matter of pronunciation there is between
Africans in Africa, and French, Spanish, Portuguese,
Italian and North Europe peoples this similarity, an
inability to make the sound *th* as in English. These
races for *th*, say *d.* Hence the patois of the plantation is *dat, dis* and *dem,* for *that, this* and *them.*
What Frenchman, born and reared in France, can

Appendix.

say *theater* as the Greeks of old or Anglo-Saxon of today, or the Arab would pronounce it? So difficult is this sound to make that, in teaching Arabic, the *that*, *d*, of Arabic has by grammarians been changed to *dal* in the Arabic grammar used in Africa.

The Anglo-Saxon Americans who were born and reared, and who lived among the blacks from infancy to old age heard the jargon or patois of the Negro in his frantic effort to overcome the hereditary limitations of his own language, more frequently than the purity of England's English spoken, and unconsciously, the provincialisms in speech of the blacks have been stamped upon the English of the South, whether Southerners (whites) would have it so — or otherwise, and the infection is upon their speech.

Herein is an anomaly, the power and influence of an inferior people over the speech of a superior race.

The word inferior is here to be taken as adventitious, and not as natural. The Negro race in America to-day is to the whites — inferior from circumstance rather than anything inherent in soul and brain. The progress already made shows this beyond cavil or controversy. Let us hope that this progress which does not make us vain, but grateful to God, is but the initial step to a better civilization than we have known.

The crudities of speech portrayed in these poems, in some, will provoke laughter, in some contempt, and not infrequently offend the sensitiveness of some; and yet they serve to remind us of the misfortunes of our ancestry and the cruelties of an alien people. But the progress made and being made by

Appendix.

us in learning convinces us that this patois is not natural to the American blacks, but simply marks the transition of African illiteracy to an alien tongue. A hundred years hence when illiteracy among the Negroes of America shall be less pronounced than it is among the masses of the whites now, this patois will prove interesting and amusing to our posterity, whose command of English and European languages will not be inferior to that of the American scholarly class of to-day.

This part of Negro tradition and history, so well preserved in verse by the muse's spirit breathed into these poems, serves to convince us that if this work is to be best done, most faithfully retained to us, the source and means must be Negro and not Caucasian.

Phyllis Wheatly of a century ago, Paul Dunbar and Daniel Webster Davis of to-day, are poets whose race identity may not be questioned, and are race representations in literature showing the world that the muses, like the gods of past ages, delight to disport themselves among the gentle Ethiopians.

JOHN H. SMYTHE.

902 Seventh street, N., Richmond, Va.

GLOSSARY.

Biggis' . . . . biggest.
Bimeby . . . . by and by.
Chana . . . . china.
Cohn . . . . corn.
Chidlins . . . . hog's entrails.
'dough . . . . although.
'dout . . . . without.
Erbout . . . . about.
Ez . . . . as.
Fhar . . . . fair.
Gallus . . . . suspender.
Gent'mun . . . . gentleman.
Gib' . . . . give.
'Gin . . . . begin.
Gimme . . . . give me.
Gwine . . . . going.
Gwy . . . . going.
Ho'ped . . . . helped.
Huccum . . . . how comes.
Hydin . . . . hydrant.
Inchin' . . . . coming slowly.
Kayed . . . . carried.
Kaze . . . . because.
Ketch . . . . catch.
Kheer . . . . care.
Kotched . . . . caught.
Lemme . . . . let me.

Glossary.

'Lijun	religion.
Marster	master.
Medjur	measure.
Mek	make.
Melojus	melodious.
Mistis	mistress.
Nat'yul	natural.
'Nogurashun	inauguration.
Nuther	neither.
Ol'	old
Patterrollers	policemen or patrolmen.
Peckin'	impose upon.
Pijin	pigeon.
Pledjur	pleasure.
Prayhr	prayer.
Ras'le	wrestle.
Reggin	reckon.
Ressin	wresting.
Roos'	roost.
Schar	scar.
Sho'	sur.
Shorz	sure as.
Speretu'l	spiritual.
Sphar	spare.
Surt'ny	certainly.
Tak' hur	get out of the way.
Tetch	touch.
Totin'	carrying.
Tredjur	treasure.
Tuther	the other.
Ub	of.
Wadermillun	watermelon.

Glossary.

Wahr	wear.
'Weh	away.
Whar	where.
Wuck	work.
Wuz	was.
Ya'll	you all.
Yer	your.
Yurz	ears.
Yuther	other.
Zerbs	deserves.